Wave IX

Other Titles from

Space Cowboy Books

Books:

Mexicans on the Moon – Pedro Iniguez

Another Time: Time Travel Stories 1942–1960

Complete Poems 1965–2020 – Michael Butterworth

Simultaneous Times Vol. 3 – Various Authors

Simultaneous Times Vol. 2.5 – Various Authors

Simultaneous Times Vol. 2 – Various Authors

Simultaneous Times Vol. 1 – Various Authors

Garbage In, Gospel Out – Jean-Paul L. Garnier

Betelgeuse Dimming – Jean-Paul L. Garnier

Future Anthropology – Jean-Paul L. Garnier

Chapbooks:

Micropoetry for Microplanets – Brian U. Garrison

Shelf Life – F. J. Bergmann

Mars Maundering – Denise Dumars

The Telepathy Machine – Jean-Paul L. Garnier

Time's Arrow – Jean-Paul L. Garnier

Utopian Problems – Jean-Paul L. Garnier

www.spacecowboybooks.com

Wave IX

Space Cowboy Books

ISBN 979-8-9896308-2-0

Edited by Jean-Paul L. Garnier

First Edition | 2024

Space Cowboy Books

61871 29 Palms Hwy.

Joshua Tree, CA 92252

www.spacecowboybooks.com

Table of Contents

In 1961 J.G. Ballard penned the story "Studio 5, The Stars," which originally appeared in *Science Fantasy* magazine. It takes place in the Vermillion Sands world and revolves around editor Paul Ransom, who runs *Wave IX*, a poetry magazine which publishes poetry generated by Verse Transcribers, or VT. A human poet intervenes, and all goes awry. The story, as much of Ballard's work, is startlingly prophetic, and today, as a poetry editor, I find myself in the inverse of this situation. Today's publishing world is filled with debates, arguments, and outright anger over the proliferation of AI/LLM/generative software created "writing" and "art" flooding the market and making editors' jobs difficult, if for no other reason that it adds mountains of garbage to the slush piles. Personally, I don't think that these machine generated works can be classified as belonging to the humanities, but since they are probably here to stay, in one form or another, I believe that we should be classifying them as "Machinities." Surely AI has its place in the sciences, on robotic space craft for instance, but do we really want it creating works of art, that which has always belonged to the human spirit? Whichever side of the debate your opinion falls on, it is fascinating that Ballard was already addressing this issue long before it came to fruition, and long before computers had entered into the daily lives of people. Science fiction has often warned of future perils, but as Ray Bradbury once said, "I don't try to describe the future, I try to prevent it." Clearly most of SF's warnings have gone unheeded.

Nevertheless, this Ballard story inspired me (as does much of his work), and so, I brought the story to many people's attention. Some were already intimately familiar, some read it for the first time. And without much explanation I asked folks to create work inspired, or related to, whatever *Wave IX* meant to them. A few of the works you will find in this publication were pre-existing, created long ago, but relevant to the theme, others were created specifically for this magazine. But I deliberately kept the prompt vague, knowing that the mind of the artist would exude originality, something which large language models by nature cannot do. I am delighted by the works that came back in response. But don't take my word for it, turn the page and decide for yourself.

Jean-Paul L. Garnier
Joshua Tree, CA
2024

Orchid Music – Jean-Paul L. Garnier

Jonathan
Nevair

The In-between Sea

by Jonathan Nevair

The message arrived, quite to my disbelief, in a bottle. It shouldn't have come as a surprise, given I was staying at a small cottage by the sea. And yet, that enigmatic missive shook me with its strangeness. Unannounced and uninvited, it returned, like the lost pages of an adventure tale, to an adolescent dreamer.

Sadly, the tremor of youthful vigor it sent through me was short lived. Soon after reading the missive, a most disturbing turn left me unable to tend to myself for many months. Only now, a year later, am I back walking among those beings of nature deemed sane and rational. And yet, my account of what transpired made sense to those with whom I conversed during my convalescence in that secluded and sheltered countryside retreat. I will recount to you, as best I can, the strange events that shifted the otherwise unmoving foundation that I call reality.

I'd taken my daily walk an hour early, suffering as I did from bouts of prolonged insomnia. Deep and contented sleep came rarely to me in those days. Like a reluctant muse, it taunted me in the crepuscular moments between waking and dreaming. Obstinate in its refusal, the ghostly form remained inches from my grasp, unwilling to lead me into oneiric slumber.

In those despairing nights on the coast, I lay with eyes shut, intent on letting go into the void of sleep. My listlessness spawned a looping mental cinema. Lucid narratives rivaling the most artful terrors of the surrealists manifested before my inner eyes, marvelous nightmares as potent as those conjured with paint and brush.

So, it came as no surprise that I was up early the day the missive chose to make its introduction. Once satisfied with tea and my pipe, I took to the morning papers, content to sit for an hour at the small breakfast table. Despite an earnest determination to read, my gaze drifted from the printed pages to the window. Twenty minutes on, I relinquished my endeavor to stay informed of the latest news and granted an uncanny impulse the freedom to pursue an unknown urge.

Thus, did I find myself strolling the strand. Infinity could be content on that lonely stretch of coastline, empty at that hour save for a stray gull scanning the nightly storm's leftovers strewn along the tide's edge.

It was then that a dull blue glint caught my eye. Like a tiny sapphire rolling on rippling velvet, it broke the beautiful monotony of the emerald sea. I watched the bottle roll up and back into the surf as if in a dream. The ebb and flow of crashing waves pushed and pulled at the small crystal castaway. I approached slowly, hypnotized by its pendulum motion. The sea's languid persistence gnawed at me until anxiety to capture the object hastened my pace. The green water continued its struggle with relentless determination. I sensed its desire to expel the corruption and yet, I knew it couldn't evict the object without assistance. Thus, my purpose that April morning became clear to me. The sea had called me for this very reason.

Chill, water-soaked sand recorded my barefooted steps as I braved the early spring waters, timing my attempts to clutch the rolling bottle with the up and back motion of the waves. Wishing to avoid the heavy report of a breaker, I danced on tiptoes to pull the mysterious message from the sea. Eventually my desire to remain dry was relinquished as futile, and I succumbed to two or three surges that drenched my linen pants but earned me the prize. I walked back to dryer sand through the inch-deep remnants of the rising tide as it rushed back into the sea. The gentle sheen of water had erased my previous presence along the shoreline while my back was turned, as if I had never been there at all.

I stood, bottle in hand, alone on a stretch of white sand. Only the rattling of a Cessna interrupted the cadence of the sea as it passed from north to south, fighting the headwind of an overcast and lonely gray sky. My eyes went from the blue glass to the passing plane, curious if the pilot was its author. An illogical thought, I soon realized, unless they had flown by that morning and dropped it like a sounding buoy a short distance into the waves. More convincing evidence to the contrary was found on the bottle's appearance. It had the look of the sea about it, like a galleon that had seen the harsh sun of the tropics and the cold and bitter currents of the northern seas.

Wet and chilled from the thighs down, I sat and examined the wandering artifact. Through the hazy glass, I found what appeared to be a rolled parchment. Instinctually, my head went north and south, scanning the strand. Was this a prank, as if Defoe or Stevenson were playing a trick from the grave? Calling on that all-too-wished-for youthful dream to cross into the unknown, get lost, and traverse the uncharted? Only the hum of the Cessna and the soaring stray gull were audible and visible suspects, and as prior evidence suggested, both were unlikely and frankly, impossible culprits.

How long had this missive been among the waves, lucky enough to survive without leaking cork or cracking glass? Had either happened, its journey would have been a meandering descent into the ocean's deep like Rimbaud's famous boat, lost forever to the belly of the sea.

In pirate fashion, I tore free the cork with biting teeth and aimed the bottle so the parchment slid out into my palm. A mild jab to my skin followed, and I quickly realized its source: the tip of a No. 2 pencil. Hidden inside the rolled paper, it emerged to my great confusion. Was a question to be answered? I unrolled the paper. To my disappointment, a blank field with no prompt or other markings stared back at me.

What deviant, what seducer of anticipation was behind this terrible hoax? My anger rose and I tossed the mischievous parchment on the sand. My attempt to break the pencil was thwarted by physics, the stem too short for my available strength, so I flung it punitively next to the paper and stared at the sea.

In time my temper simmered, and although I eyed the bottle and its contents with occasional malice, the ocean's expanse pulled my mind to other possibilities. A castaway perhaps, driven mad through isolation and the struggle for survival? Or an unlucky person, kidnapped with hopes of sending a desperate message, forced through unfortunate serendipity by an arriving captor to simply dispose of the evidence by tossing it overboard. How delightfully awful a thought. Or had something been written on that empty page and lost to the ages as the bottle floated for years, decades even, on the high seas at the mercy of the solar rays?

In due time I found myself conjuring further imaginings. The tabula rasa of this strange treasure expelled from the sea prompted my mind to crack an unsolvable mystery. After an hour of this futile activity, I resigned myself to hunger and made my way up to the small rental for lunch. Without thinking, I picked up the bottle, paper, and pencil and took it with me. I had always been one to avoid littering and intended to put all three in the rubbish bin.

An hour later, content at the kitchen table having lunched, I stared at the bottle, paper, and pencil. They sat beyond my empty plate, interrupting the view through the window of the sea. Having survived my resentment and, through some unknown compassion, all three items had managed to accompany me into the house. If anything, the guilty party was the bottle. The age and weathered appearance twisted my conscience, as if I was abandoning an elderly relative in need.

The trio served as companion for dinner that night, having lain stationary at the table during the in-between hours in respite from the years alone at sea. I am sure the bottle enjoyed that stillness. Endless days of constant motion most likely gave it the same sickly disequilibrium we suffer after boating, kitchen swaying left and right in a bodily hallucination, grappling with the sudden change to circumstance.

As the sun set, I smoked my pipe and eyed the paper and pencil. What had been the purpose of this provocation? To take childish excitement and distort its purpose to an empty gesture of disappointment? Out of a growing desire to reinstate balance in the universe, I grabbed the paper and pencil. I scribbled a line, stuffed it in the bottle and found a suitable cork from a half-empty bottle of Merlot and capped the top.

In minutes I was at the water's edge, bottle in hand. To anyone back at the line of houses along the dunes I would have appeared like an imbibing loner, embracing the sunset with a salty gesture of locality. The ebbing tide made for perfect conditions to return the bottle to the sea, and I leisurely followed a retreating wave to its farthest drawback and hurled the glass. For the next half hour, I sat and stared as it drifted to a distant speck, vanishing in the fading light of the surrealist hour of waking. Or was it sleeping?

A difficult night followed. Storms which loomed at the horizon made their long-awaited appearance. Lightning, rain, and high seas filled the world outside my bedroom window. Had I angered the waters with my response? Were the spirits of the deep insulted by my written question? Or could this be mere chance, the bottle tossing about on hostile crests by nothing other than arbitrary natural forces and the insignificant act of a lone and idle traveler?

I woke late, finding sleep at last in the late hours of the night. By the time I'd eaten, smoked, and read the morning paper, the bottle was only mildly perturbing my senses. An occasional glance at the empty space on the table where it had been the night previous barely prodded my balanced mood. I intended to avoid the beach that morning, as the storm had made for an uninviting mess of seaweed, shells, and driftwood along the strand. But then I caught sight of a family out the window heading north, investigating the flotsam and jetsam. A strange urgency rose within me. I hastened out and down to the shoreline, frantic to reach the edge of the water in front of the house before their imminent arrival.

As I neared the storm's debris, the youngest of the group, a lad of no more than four or five, reached down into a muck of seaweed and extracted an item. I longed to call out a warning, but he was too far south for my voice to reach him. The boy held in his hand the itinerant bottle. He ran to his companions and displayed the item, offering it to one of the adults. She took it and quite to my shock and surprise, threw it out into the sea. The child reacted as expected, disappointed to a degree bordering on trauma.

Why deny such youthful joy? Again, my temper flared. I intended to make for the approaching party when my eye was drawn to the glint of blue glass. The bottle pitched about in knee-deep water, moving outward into the sea. The walking party came about and began a retreat in the southerly direction. I eyed the bottle. It proceeded further out into the waves.

The boy turned, hand clasped by his parent, and cast a last glance at the lost treasure before acquiescing to parental authority. I stared for what must have been several minutes. By the time I caught the scent of my waking state they were growing small, like the distant figures in an uncanny dream.

Fleeting relief washed over me. I recalled what I had written in the bottle and the dark horrors rose to cast a shadow over my small victory. Angry and resentful words penciled on the paper in the bottle would have been as traumatizing to the child's eyes as the denial of their parent's access to its contents. Anxiety and embarrassment rose as traumatic twins, and I dashed into the surf. I bounded through the breakers, ignoring the frigid water, to retrieve the bottle. Every stroke was like a taunt, and it pulled away from me, drifting farther out into the sea. Kicking and splashing, I swam with gusto, but soon the temperature slowed my progress. My breathing grew short and tight. I turned, frantic, to check my distance to the shore. The sight of white sand rising and falling in and out of view as the breakers crashed drew forth a new horror. I was being pulled, with the bottle, out to sea. I waved and shouted, aiming my pleas and gestures in the direction of the family receding to the south. None turned. The hum of the returning Cessna lay distant to the north, a mere dot at the milky horizon. My body rose and fell on the swells as if in a gentle caress. I turned to seek the bottle. It bobbed in synchronized rhythm with me, remaining out of arm's reach.

Again and again, I cried out, my pleas growing fainter as the sea's distance to the shoreline stretched like elastic. Tiring, the haunting reality of my situation revealed itself and I embraced the silent victory of the sea. With a last effort I kicked and spun, saltwater violating my inward gasps. That first taste of the end stung and also drew forth the quiet deep of a sleeping sea. To the south, I caught sight of the walking party and the one who threw the bottle, the parent who had so brazenly and heartlessly denied a child the serendipitous adventure of youth.

I waved a desperate hand and called out. She turned and looked out to sea and I recognized the face of my mother.

The above transcript was recorded during the narcoleptic memory sessions of Alfred Merriweather, patient of Dr. Louise Hurst at the Fairton Downs Psychiatric Clinic. Date: May 4th, 1948.

Day of Sacrifice – Aaron Sheppard

F.J. Bergmann

Colors in the Air

by F.J. Bergmann

blue cornfields again
azure leaves drooping miserably
another MicroDoleNestApplZon product campaign

old Mrs. (Mrs.!) Bellatra's garden
dyed Pink™ to celebrate her son's wedding
sued into the next millennium

boardroom rage at red-tide ubiquity
since climate catastrophe—risk of losing
rights to a trademark hue

big weatherbiz controlling storms
and rainbows—cloud-painting
license fees keep going up

economic balance—credit for inclusion
of corporate logos offset by surcharge
for use of proprietary colors

less vandalism than expected
natural clouds too high for drones—
FAA surveillance bots target the rest

customer-survey-driven prompts
for AI cloud-painting patterns to inspire poems
(also AI): endless loop

a horde of anarchist balloons rise silently
into the night—dawn greets a green skyscape
of floating forest islands

Eugen
Bacon

A Beautiful Paean

by Eugen Bacon

The poems happened one Friday evening when Reef installed a pilot AI module into his footy app. Shitty little verses took over his device and the match center on his screen was stuffed. He lost the fixtures and results, no running ticker with the latest news feed.

When he clicked to look at the live ladder, who was who, where they were positioned and by how many points high or low, all he saw was a flickering ode named 'Perfectly Portioned' in its stead. It was about a sensible car and a crucial crux.

Wow, just wow. Nothing good about the wow.

Reef wanted to see how the Servals were doing. The Lynxes. The Caracals. The Ocelots. The Pantheras. The Cougars. The Cheetahs. The Leopards. A week of games had passed, and this shifted scores for winners and losers.

Last he looked, his team, the Sokokes, was top five on the ladder. They'd played 11 games, earned 36 points. The Cougars were on the leaderboard at 40 points. But now there was no live score or leaderboard—just those awful, fragmented sonnets.

And he hated poems! One was called 'Body Up', and it went like this:

~

Silence blots out the jay's cheh, bubble, rattle.

The telly wobbles then

unmutes itself louder than normal.

A journo tells between gasping

the woes of a slashing
inside a mall in broad
daylight right in the belly of the city.
No image, head or gesture
—just snow and lines on the screen
a scarlet spatter.
No closed captions
or ticker scroll. Just an aftermath.
The future is here.

~

Reef looked at the next poem, 'Things You Don't Fret About When You're A Ghost,' and his head hurt. His skull was full of bees, no honeycombs in it. The buzzZZZ was as insistent as it was industrious.

The hell?

He clicked on the icon that was meant to show who was playing, but instead of team by day and the stadium they were at, the screen wobbled and recited at him in a posh English voice, a bloke's at that, the worst ballad whose text also displayed on the screen:

~

Ode to An Alphabet of No Can Do

… motivation ≤ on hold?
… hierarchy of needs [^ to the power of joy in €]
… echoes of an ©ppressive past
… fated? [full time helper™]
… inequality ☺? / noun: inhumane
… junior ®? / adj: sub- or lesser
… kitchen hand?
… more tolerable ☺?
… puppet ☺?
… queening out ≥ queening?
*… take it for the team? * the direction never changes*
… uh … um … [beaten back × ∞ infinity]
… victim? that's just reality
… no? (encore)
… yes ^ ∑verything?
… equality? = no rights

~

Reef wished it was an ad, but it wasn't. It was a dreadful poem. He thought of many places he could tell it to go, one of which comprised a bodily orifice. Where were the footy videos—the ones showing his favorite match scorer Bonza fashioning a banana, a beautiful kick that turned the game over, put the Sokokes higher on the leaderboard?

He'd give anything to hear a siren, the start or close of a footy match.

He looked at the AI-smorgasbord with a strained smile—a smile because what was he supposed to do: cry? He'd walk out on the bloody thing if he could, but the phone crooned a dancy tune all moony, so flirty, it held him at ransom for a moment.

Nup, he had enough of it. He switched the phone off.

But, even without lights, it was alive. It trembled in his hands and proclaimed, "Good kick, I reckon. Thump it long, Reef. I'd say it's average. Here's a counterattack!"

Then, to his chagrin, the phone switched itself back on, displayed a scoreboard for a minute. He scrolled up, up. Sokoke… Sokoke… "How we doing?" he spoke to himself. The match report faded out and another terrible poem blinked full vim on the screen. This one was called "Laugh and Go", and the first stanza was about smart play out front in a game of chaos.

Bloody unbelievable. He nearly cried.

He turned on the telly. But footy was not on free-to-air. He was a cheapskate. Who wouldn't be with the income he got at that dumb-assed job? Yep. No streaming service on the big screen of his one bedroomed apartment. Nothing to give him direct feedback from roaring commentators. No pulsing crowd at some grandstand in Wagga Wagga, Joy Joy or Woop Woop.

So he vacuumed the raggedy carpet, years showing on its pale-green threads. It swallowed up enough fluff to choke up a casket. He made himself a cuppa. Weak—three drops of skimmed milk. He called it dirty tea. He sank in moroseness on the couch and watched the news about some billionaire's scandal—sex, money and whatever it was that got rich people in a pickle. Then he watched a doco about entrepreneurs in the Sahara investing in camel wool for high fashion design, proceeds of which went to feed the children, donate antibiotics and anesthesia to flying doctors in war-torn countries. News and documentaries instead of thrumming footy. There was no ball turnover. No crowds full house on the grandstands, screaming heartiness or rudeness as best-on-the-field Bonza got out of a tackle, executed an instant 180 with his body, the opposition coming at him, numbers everywhere… Bonza side-stepping, dribble, dribble… Goal!

Commentators bellowing: "He's a delightful kick!"

There was none of that.

Reef stepped out to his balcony and stared long and hard at the blinking white stars far high in the black sky. He was scared to go to sleep. What if he woke and found poems writing themselves on his walls? Formless, plague-like things. Vomiting themselves. On the white ceiling, on open and shut doors, inside the vegetable compartment in the fridge... What if he peered at the microwave and, inside it, and everywhere he looked, was a bloody poem?

***

He woke to a quiet apartment. No poems on the walls or ceilings or doors, or anything like that. He restarted his smartphone and it uncharacteristically said his name on reboot.

"Oh, good on ya, Reef. Where's your sense of occasion?"

This was an emergency. The world was coming to an end. But he knew it was just the phone. That pilot AI module installation.

He considered chucking the device into the toilet. He actually started walking towards the bathroom—not an ensuite. Just then, the phone startled him with a querulous *tu-a-wee* chime of bluebirds. It barely lasted a second, then it piped, "The future isn't what it is, Reef. Is it?"

Ruin my life in a week, he thought.

"Already on it!" merrily sang the smartphone, as if hearing his innermost thoughts, and Reef and his feelings bottomed out.

"Skipper, don't be like that," said the phone, getting his pessimistic vibe.

***

Reef thought it through the whole morning. He vacuumed and drank cup after cup of tea, ignoring Jamilla's texts: *You're late.* Then: *Are you gonna effin show?* Darn. It was Monday already. No weekend footy was there to give him much-needed respite from his marketing consultancy job and its broom-up-the-ass boss.

He contemplated calling in sick, but was too distracted.

He picked his phone and, on afterthought, uninstalled the footy app.

He shoved the device into his pocket. Reached into the fridge and grabbed a tinny. He cracked it open and Buddy beer frothed on his tongue. He sank back on the couch in the lounge, turned the telly on and, oh, goody, what do you know? There was his team on a match replay—the Pantheras unable to stop the bleed.

Striker Bonza won a scramble, put some speed on his feet. He was a whole sprinting machine, kicking as he ran, found Horn-Francis, flicked the ball at full range. Somehow, the footy was back at his feet.

Commentators yelling, "Bonza! Bonza!"

"He's a reliable man in front of the sticks."

Snap, goal!

"He's a very reliable man!"

This was more like it. Reef seduced himself into the game, watched as his fave caressed the ball through the posts.

A Panthera rookie flounced the ball off his foot but it went nowhere, and the crowd guffawed. Then wonder Bonza was there in a flash. A kick right at the fifty mark on the field got Reef and the crowd roaring.

Victory was sweet. The Sokokes would be higher up, up the ladder. He was tempted for a moment to install the footy app. But the poems…

Only now they had infiltrated his mind. Words were shaping in his head, something about driving and lilies. A song of bluebirds.

The hell?

And Armageddon was happening in his pocket. The device vibrated, leapt and boomed: "Turn the game over! Fifteen intercepts! Spread it wide! That's *not* a beautiful kick!"

He felt it doing an Incredible Hulk against his thigh, cried out loud as it tore through the pants, leaped onto his hands, and it was no longer a smartphone. It was a friggin tablet-sized device.

"Goal!" it chimed, hurled itself at the telly, *smash, smash,* then swirled back intact into his hands, as the TV shattered onto his exhausted carpet.

"No, no. No!" Reef yelled at it. He wrenched the lunatic thing off his body, but it grabbed at him with invisible hands.

"You're in a bit of a mood," the tablet said. "Try not to be so defensive."

He wrestled with it until, winded, he gave up.

Now the tablet snuggled at Reef's chest. "That was a blinder. Don't do it again," it said. He stared at it, wordless. "Mate, we don't do that," it cooed. "Be a team. Easy now, let me give you a beautiful paean." And it recited a replay in that all-blokey and posh Pommy voice:

~

Things You Don't Fret About When You're A Ghost

an apartment
lit with hand-painted watercolurs vases and photos
memories in a frame   a smart screen right there 7-inch screen
you'll never make a cuppa   vanilla chai   one minute in the microwave
milk just right   now look at the bills

a toilet seat

practical   engineered for a use   works on gravity

it's not to eat breakfast / check your emails   just a healthy disposal unit

takes what you shed   save you from a megacolon

how long   can you go without

a box of tissues

crumbs of sourdough   drools of soup

knows skin and bums   feet and cheeks

it's not a letter from the bank   a copy of your life insurance

just a box of tissues   unremembered on your coffee table

a ridex

sometimes on time sometimes it isn't   you don't know what you get

but you can cancel the fare   one driver asks do you want water

takes you to a destination   rates you out of five

you rate them back   put flame lilies on your tombstone

an airport

hosts in immaculate caps   here's your boarding pass

travel information   declarations   restrictions that apply

all you think is hotspots   not the WI-FI kind

there's not enough runway

a swimming pool

azure water ebony lines sunlit rays through a glassy roof

a bench you never sit on a silent clock tick tock tick tocking as you dive

mostly you're alone bubbles as you breathe shimmers on the lanes

dead lizard on the floor water's ruffled when you leave

~

Reef stared at the ode, aghast and in resignation. What astonished him even more was that an original poem was shaping itself on his mind. He couldn't believe it, how natural the verse found access to his brain and thought itself out in lower case:

~

what to banish

can be milestones
or untruths
as you drive
in just a minute
through lilies
at the wake
tu-a-wee chime
the bluebirds/
the coffin's
a ripper.

~

Just then the tablet wobbled.

Reef looked at the screen and, slowly, his finger hovered—as if on its own volition—over a flashing icon: *Install now: Footy Pro AI 2.0.*

Faces of Ballard – Jean-Paul L. Garnier

Michael

Butterworth

Concentrate 1

by Michael Butterworth

Fragments of a Letter Found in a Dead Astronaut's Possessions

Takeoff: fumed and awful gravity pull.

I am leaving earth forever.

Time: cancelled by this crave for sexual desire. Streaming grey matter from the nose.

Hands: blood things filmed with cellophane, centred bone, dying edges of some bleak being.

Granular images blocked in the electric dark of my skull. Space is a vast church, though no people have any connection with it, or if they had they would fall out of time.

Space is a matrix of avenues, cold planes of continuity. Human feature is blurred by the spiralling patterns of space, rendered insignificant by their continual cone formation and wave within wave fluctuation. It becomes an inverted reassemblement of its actual makeup, a highway of space and its sized, ever-changing globular designs.

I am in a presence. Space is composed of these continually blended, interplaying phases of itself – an incident within presence.

I'm drained of time. A sperm floating. A haze of tears, where hard stones are the stars.

Deep Freeze Unit for Hungry Spacers

The moon was out shining. Some strange animals had made a nest in his beard. A bolt cracked the mirror in two parts so he could see the landscape below stretched pink into the distance.

Clalvalar started running away, screaming as the temperature rose:

"I'M THE DEEP FREEZE MAN – THE DEEP FREEZE MAAAANNN ————————" Soon landscape responded to his call and it darted red-hot points of light on to his quavering body. Responded and sent him staggering to top speed over the white-hot rocks. Into the dark green cloudland land of night where the pink sun never had its chance. Into the cold and purple lozenge of his deep-freeze unit.

The planet had woken – seven shades from dawn.

From the tops of the deep freeze unit he could see the tops of monsters lumbering into the green dark of the planet's other half.

Clalvalar's unit was buckled below the black fingerless hulk of Deep Freeze itself. He depressed a lever.

From under the cavernous mouth of Deep Freeze two wide rivers began to run. The rivers branched into countless thousands of parallel channels spreading a clawed hand over the entire sunny side – thawing food – depositing it for use at the tops of tall feeder towers.

Black stainless flies, attracted by the adverts in space, buzzed around and settled magnetically clamped to the towers and rose after feeding. Clalvalar began to scream. Amplifiers shrieked out of hand from all points of the planet: “I'M THE DEEP FREEZE MAN – THE DEEEP FREEEZE MAAAANNN———————— ”

“The Deeeepp Freeeeezzzze Maaaaaannn————” Contraption picked up and pierced out in its tiny high voice.

Contraption controlled Frozen Foods as they drifted swiftly under its bulk, draining noises from the air. Deadly and sick machine worked inside its sprawled gut spraying gamma rays from its gulf belly.

The green night advanced the slow rumbling of the monsters and spun the world round.

Clalvalar plunged up the lever and was left in silence.

He ran out to catch the trade cold and the frozen noise of splitting rocks in the green night. The last to linger round the towers were the regulars.

The Catalogue of the Works of Man

A sharp outlined final landscape – privileged. Nothing like it had met up with me before.

The Automobile was not a part of the landscape as I was a part of the brain landscape.

The Automobile sprang into focus. For a moment the buildings of the car of the Man slotted into place, then fell apart dreaming.

I got in.

Red cab rolling silently off. It was a sharp-outlined final landscape. I caught sight of the Artist pottering about amongst the rubble.

"OK?" he said, drawing near. "Blueblack or blue-black, take your pick."

"Oh, an awful lot of nothing. A lead on the singer Ringo Starr maybe or a crossriddle to hell. Was he? Or maybe no good. I can't get these straight lines. Ads all over the place. Difficult to follow. Maybe if we tried the old library?"

(Remembered seeing the Palace Theatre. And further up the road the round bearable dome of the Manchester Public Library.)

"No records there. I checked. Blueblack stains on the walls. Some fungus in all that silence or now the Stones are coming!"

As we talked the last clouds were coiling fantastically within the Wave. Wave of substance and dark culture. Leftovers of the white bones of the Men – silent curlers creeping into the unknown substance of the concrete chips, clipped together with hairpin fragments of bone. Only the sun made a noise as it set behind the clouds – a sucking sound.

"The City," I shot a death hand over silence and hung clouds over the City.

A hole in the ground sent firmly a shit eye to stare up at me forever. Several soft spots of sand. The last of Man and somehow very sad.

The Artist rose from where he had been, and walked away into the shadows. Blackness within made me stay late in the last night, sifting sand through old and electric but fine.

The morning.

I swallowed.

I turned into the City.

I sat in the dark for hours as the sun rose.

After Galactic War, from a Road on Earth

The road wound along under the night sky. Set in the sky were the crystals of the ships that had broken. Each chip was a silent last fleck of humanity. Together with the vanity of the ground that bent up to meet them the space beyond buckled inwards under the pressure of the true stars and sandwiched the chips into bars of space music. They needed no air – were the archaic flowers off the rings of all dead girls. Gems centred the jewelled scene into curls in the front of my head.

I looked out of the forehead of a double-decker bus and my legs were wheels. I rolled over the pitted road pickpocketing the night. I rode the night like a baby stalk lost in Heaven not seven, anymore, wondering why.

To Be Read Indifferently

Adverts come and adverts go and if you're lucky they'll make an impression. I tried to make a really vivid impression upon myself before the War Atomic Agoraphobia Maniacs overtook the planet. A Heinz bean-can label, for instance, makes a world of difference to your reasoning power – it virtually dulls it out. And those are the mental conditions you/I kind of wanted when we realised the end was at hand.

•

With grateful acknowledgements to the late JG Ballard, who edited this from my much longer text.

Carter
Kaplan

The Nanopoetic Quest in Theory and Practice

by Carter Kaplan

THE STARS LOOKED A LITTLE TOO real. I was hoping for a more striking impression. "Bright points in an inky ether" or "burning hosts of scintillating suggestion casting their long lances down against a suppliant earth" or "silver fathers of insight populating a multiverse with daughters of illusion." No. It was just stars above me. But the landscape was stimulating—a vast desert of pentagonal tiles, widely spaced groups of motionless palms, tufts of bent and still reeds, delicate skeletal flowers stretched tall and fossilized, boulders strewn about with agreeable randomness. Far off was a horizon described in places by the sullen glow of distant cities—with tremendous voids, nearly perfectly black, between those cities, if that's what they were. The blushes of light could have been the glowing of setting moons, or the exteriorization of the sullen brooding of fanatical devils dancing around bonfires for burning witches, or maybe something more important. The brush strokes of an important artist who had caught the attention of a Peggy Guggenheim, a Gertrude Vanderbilt Whitney, a Lizzie Bliss... About a mile off was a two-lane highway whose concrete surface was playfully animated by the headlights of Cardiacs, Stinkrays, whizzing bi-wheel café razors and revving ratrods.

In the distance, receding, looming, shifting, stabilizing, I saw a stone and glass-walled house suggesting the cover of a glossy architecture magazine. Every line and corner made a statement. Massive yet closely hugging the tiled desert, it was a single-story home framed in stone and metal. Glass walls stretched from the ground to a flat and slightly-sloping roof. I was at a bit of a quandary, as the house reflected both the agreeable tastes of designer Stewart Williams but also something of the vulgarity of the entertainers who had commissioned him to force his visions into the coarse purposes of mere *pleasureteria*. I could hear the thwack and spring of a diving board, a splash, a trickle of voices, the intermittent chattering of indistinct personas punctuated with slips of silence and an occasional bravura of laugher. Music came on—the high-fidelity recording of one of those professional Burbank orchestras executing the crisp conga-infused anthem of a tiki lounge soiree, swinging flute pips and trills, expert, precise, lyrical arpeggios running across the polyrhythms… but now as the wind rose and shifted, it sounded like tin, an increasing sense of distance, then shifting and rushing up with a sharply-attenuated proximity in the sudden stillness and clear emptiness of the slowly chilling night. I struck off toward the music, my trusty anorak draping from my shoulders like a cape.

The tiles I placed my feet upon were those old sand-rays, flattened, stretched, skewed, forming an Escher-like lattice of interlocking pentagonal flags. Long ago they had been drawn down from the air—as I recalled, remembering the brochure—shaped, hardened, set together in a mosaic that occasionally adjusted itself with heaves and shivers, restoring a nostalgic sense of space, a softly-rolling desert, a vacant range where people could be alone to indulge the impression of a private demesne, the elegant luxury of a field of one's own, a personal *Lebensraum* at long last. The sand-paper surface softly scrapping beneath my boots sounded authentic enough. The minuscule tooth-like plates cladding the sand-ray skin—what substituted in sharks and rays for fishes' scales—was a good place to find nanopoems, I felt sure of it.

My boots scraped along slowly, and I noticed my progress was stilted, so that intermittently I compared myself to Alice running and getting nowhere, but instead of running and getting nowhere I was *walking* and getting nowhere. I appreciated that. Why put forth extra effort to achieve the same result?

The rock and glass-walled house was still far off; distance self-adjusting to accommodate the fluctuating objectives of my attention. Catching my breath and producing my torch and magnifying lens, I stooped down to look for one of those poems. Beneath the enlarging glass the dermal denticles instantly flashed into relief—that is, they became delightfully discernable like an inversion of the good old "disorder in the dress"—and as my torchlight played about, I thrilled to behold the shadows cast around that lattice of evenly and consistently interlocking pentagons wonderfully reflecting, in microcosm, the interlocking sand-rays covering the desert. Compare the monarch of the sky mirrored in wanton Arethusa's azur'd arms. Here was a realm where the *suspension of disbelief* and its mistress *verisimilitude* were hardly foci for consideration. Without effort I conceived myself stepping slowly—indeed *plodding*, hairs on the nape of my neck bristling—as I made my way through that denticle forest, gradually turning the torch light before me, shining it into the shadows, peeking around the V-shaped pedestals supporting the flattened tops of the pentagons recapitulating each other in the canopy above, raising my ear toward the shadows, again sweeping my torch-beam to marvel at the consistency of the spacing among the repeating forms of bending pedestals defined among the bands of moving light and turning shadow; I half expected to encounter a moiré effect, but nothing.

Some time passed in this way, nothing presented itself, and so I reasoned prudence behooved me to resume my stroll to the rock and glass-walled house.

The path was virtually untrodden; indeed, it was the proverbial (and hence venerable) road not taken. I picked up stones and cast them before me into the darkness, occasionally prompting a rattlesnake to rattle, whereupon I carefully altered my course and proceeded around the horrid creature toward my goal—my good-natured expectations, disabused of distracting aspirations, trippingly along with my tongue coming off with me, as a machine might phrase it.

The house loomed up, sill larger, and loomed up some more as I approached. In the light of perhaps three-score tiki torches the rock foundation, broad planar chimney, cantilevered horizontal accents, and the lightweight-yet-stolid pillars rising between the glass walls appeared first gray and then beige, laced though with many linear striations, subtly-latticed grains, and gorgeous pigmentations. Steel mullions and breeze blocks wonderfully accentuated the structure, which, attending my delta perspective, radiated impressions of cantilevered surfaces and horizontal inflections. In the glass the tiki torches flickered like snake tongues, the double panes producing double tongues suggesting dual valiances—an obvious allusion to the Temple of Delphi and the Pythian priestess enthroned before the holy tripod from whence the smoldering laurel sent forth wending smoke, and, in turn, through the priestess came the ambiguous prophecies of Apollo, who had slain the forked-tongued python and so gained the misty powers of second-sight.

And the beautiful music drew me forward.

As I paced with an easy and leisurely swagger, and then rapidly stepped onto the expansive, multi-level sand-ray-flagged patio that surrounded the pool, I was struck to discover the small orchestra was not a recording but was an actual Burbank orchestra. The flautist was fabulous in her gossamer gown, her golden armlets, her thick blonde hair floating like the bucolic notes from her silver instrument—and she wore a diamond tiara! She was most attractive, and I filed this away. I wondered about the resources of the host, whoever it might be. Here was the ground zero of mid-century modern design. Who could conceive such a pile, much less build it? Obviously a zillionaire! But even more striking was the fact that the first group I came upon (sitting in chaise lounge chairs, sporting fashionable swimwear, and kept warm by the ample tiki torches) was engaged in a lively discussion about *me*.
Admittedly, the evidence for saying so was not ample, but upon entering I heard one of them grumbling about "That damn editor, he's cut off so many heads with his ax—" Catching sight of me, the speaker abruptly ceased talking, while a person with his back to me interjected in posh

English strains: "An ax? He's rather got it down to a science and uses a guillotine!" But upon registering that his *bon mot* had not produced the expected guffaws, he shifted in his chair, turned fully, and discovered in my mild form his painful lack of discretion. He glared at me with explosive alarm. Turning white as a ghost and not knowing what else to do, he abruptly sprang from his chaise lounge, extended his arms before him, pawed with slapping feet across the flags with his arms held fixed in that ridiculous attitude, and dived into the pool. He had a fine form; I'll give him that. The others stood staring at each other, now and then shifting glances toward me with mixed reluctance, scorn, and abject fear. I sought to ease the tension:

"Never mind me, kids. I'm just here to read the meter."

I raised my elbows in a bouncy pantomime of a lively jog and, grinning broadly, initiated a stroll to the open glass entry with a large tawny cat suddenly appearing and bounding before me.

At the other side of the entrance was a large floor-to-ceiling mirror, and seeing himself the big Tom turned sideways, arched his back, fluffed up his tail and the hairs along his spine, froze, lifted his left forepaw, froze again, then shifted his feet slightly as he skirted first backward and then forward, froze once more, flicked his tongue at his own nose… It came to him like a revelation. Discovering that the cat in the mirror mocked his own movements, he recalled what the mirror was and who that was in the mirror, so he suddenly sat and began patiently licking his paw as his spine hairs settled back into place. The tail remained fluffed, however, and I correctly surmised it would be necessary for him to lick those hairs down when he was fully himself, which anyway he would be soon; then, as I predicted, he began licking the fur on his tail.

I would have stood there (maybe looking foolish, I didn't care) admiring the cat, if I wasn't suddenly bumped into by a self-driving Hararicart shoving a drink into my hands. I took it. It looked like Scotch. I tasted. It was Scotch, and a fine single malt it was indeed!

And it was an expensive single malt. Again, I found myself wondering about the host. Who was throwing this shin-dig? I was also wondering about the flautist, as the band was then taking a break.

But now a rather thin and sophomoric-looking young man stepped up to speak with me. He was dressed for a literary affair—at least he wore clothes suggesting a young person's impression of what to wear to a literary affair. Specifically, he was dressed in the dandified sartorial smashup of an off-the-rack Oscar Wilde. Everything was small and close-fitting, excessively trimmed with patterned ribbon and embroidery. He was a conflagration of purple, blue and gold: a velvet sack coat, an azure cravat and floppy white bow-tie, velvet waist-jacket (purple again, but sufficiently off-color to suggest carelessness), a dark carnelian shirt (silk), and tight short-breeches falling around his knees, where creased and crumpled hose carried the theme down his calves. Fashioned of very thin leather, his black slippers looked rather feeble, not cheap but wholly impractical. In the lapel of his coat he sported a lily, and of course he was carrying a small sunflower that, evidently, had become superfluous. As he spoke he repeatedly slapped the thing against his hand. I vaguely wondered if he might have brought a date, and I looked around for someone resembling Virgina Woolf.

I knew I was in for a tiresome tirade of one kind or another. He didn't disappoint as he informed me who his professor was, and how his professor disapproved my many "safe" positions. Whether he (or his professor) was referring to my politics or my editorial judgments, I could not tell. He continued. I was a luddite—and here the young man cackled. At me? At his professor? Maybe he was simply enjoying the moment. I mumbled and raised my drink to my mouth to obscure myself yet further, and turned away. But there before me was another young key tapper who hadn't yet learned to fear a person who might be a proper judge of poetry from the perspective of taste *and* revenue streams. The former youngling (who was still laughing and declaiming behind me) was a sophomore; this new one was a postgrad. His clothing rather reflected the climate—wool socks, hiking shoes, hiking shorts, safari shirt festooned with pockets, a Stetson hat, a tangle of woven-thread bracelets on his left wrist, and he wore a red patterned kerchief around his neck, no doubt a relic from some private school or other "back East." He looked tight and vaguely angry. I would say "dissatisfied," but he seemed most satisfied with his discontent.

As I might have expected, his "offense" (directed toward me, of course) was predicated on the claim that the poetry machines represented a sort of conduit for the "new mycelium" now entering the universe, and which was communicating across multi-dimensional channels to promote a "greater love and understanding among peoples everywhere." He looked at me with pitiful gravity. "It is trying to help us."

"Have you seen that flautist?" I said, profoundly, and I raised an eyebrow with an arch meaning that was probably lost on him. "There are some lovely women at this party. How do your talking mycelium compare to them?"

Much to my chagrin, he didn't miss a beat. "Well," he said, "the women appear real enough, but there have always been cosmetics, hair dye, high heels..." and somehow his tirade shifted to something about "The continuation of the species... Obsolete now... Eternity had always been a mirage concept, very simply everything is happening *now*... Plato is right when he says... The uterus is a revolving door for digitized karma... Why, there is no longer even a need for people to load the programs; now the machines do that themselves..." Was he speaking of human procreation or making poems? I forget what else he said because I was concentrating on an exit, and indeed I raised my nearly-drained glass in his face, swirled the ice, and walked away.

I looked around again for the flautist, but a tapping conga, an alternating high-hat and snare, a softly scratching guitar, a pumping bass, tickling piano keys... then the sweet trill of the flute told me the band had resumed. At least I knew where she was.

Of course there were other women: wives, adventuresses, women seeking husbands, very attractive, all of them brilliant in one way or another. Never underestimate the intelligence of women attracted to literary gatherings, even if they are there "superficially" seeking husbands. Of course there were the other kind. I've already mentioned the Virginia Woolf types, who after all are fair enough partners once they have had a child or two and settled down. I saw the ex-wives of musicians and filmmakers, now looking for someone more stable, someone who could help with their children. Not far off, raising to inspect one of the pale pentagonal sculptures that populated the room, I saw and briefly admired the famed Vivian Darkbloom, that brilliant muse of countless screenwriters and producers. Now seeing her in person for the first time, I was able to fully tap my antennae against her chilly *habitus*. My impression of her was not disappointing, albeit awful. She strikingly appeared as one of those Lilith-like lamias drawn to literary gatherings to cause a sensation of one kind or another, maybe sitting in with the band for an impromptu "session" on the congas, and who would invariably seek further validation through a fast attachment to a decadent novelist or pimply poetaster.

Before me now stepped—and continued stepping, thank goodness—a tall fellow in a green wig, ungainly monster platform shoes, mini-skirt, trampy-looking blouse tied around enormous bosoms, his chunky face globed over with grotesque make-up and suggesting a homicidal clown... As I said he was rather tall (indeed, he was very large) and something about his bearing led me to the unsavory (and quite frankly frightening) impression that the fellow was so dressed as a provocation to create an explosive scene of mischief. Not only was his *ensemble* an expression of angry misogyny, but also it was a sort of chip-on-the-shoulder meant to provide a pretext for throwing himself into a profound rage and giving some hapless "offender" a rough beating.

At this point the crowd of guests, perhaps cold or tiring of the music, became quite tightly packed inside the room. Someone was starting a fire in the deep vacuity beneath the long marble mantle. A large trainwreck of explosive reds and bottomless blues hung above the fireplace; it was Max Ernst's "The Bird from Overseas," a rather bold statement, inappropriately dominating the room, as rather than compliment the bright and open space it all but *wrecked into* the pale beige myliobatiformes sculpture and white walls, and thuggishly struggled for attention with the black and beige paddles of the slowly-turning mobile off toward the bar... but as the people packed together the colors were subdued in the increasing homogeneity of the scene. The faces of the guests lost what little identity they had brought with them; packing personae wove together in a lattice of confused conversation. The party was reaching its peak, or so it seemed.

The competing voices grew louder. I am no expert on the psychology of crowds, but it was evident the compressed humanity affected everyone with the need to be heard. It grew louder still. My anorak was slipping down my right arm, so I tugged at the lapel, restoring the garment over my shoulders. I finished my drink and planned a path to the patio to ogle the flautist and her floating hair.

Then I was accosted by another one—one of the machine people, or rather another champion of the machine and its new poetry. His face wore the expression of everyone in that faceless discorporate crowd; in turn, his voice was the voice of that fashionable crowd, and the voice was waxing in the optative mood, underscoring the disjointed nature of experience, declaiming cause and effect, sort of a modern Hume in this way, enthralled in a rhapsody concerning the disconnectedness of experience, the lack of continuity to human perceptions, a sort of frame-by-frame disjointedness insinuating a kind of neo-animism in which each nanopoem was a universe separate and distinct among an infinity of likewise separate and distinct universes, the world in a grain of sand, eternity in a flower, and so on. I shuddered, and speaking to no one I pronounced, "This one's off on a comet with Leibniz."

He was dressed in business casual; unimaginative, nondescript and "safely homogenized." I found myself wondering about his antecedents. These days even clerks were calling themselves poets. Maybe this was harsh, but I was just then jostling under the throes of a sudden "vision" of the great number of people I did not know who yet knew me. It might have been that this one-sided familiarity had inspired his growing forcefulness as he lectured: "As a matter of fact, consciousness not only infects objects, but institutions as well. Indeed, each official practice is overseen by a distinct grammatical typology…" As he drew deeper into his dissertation on the new animism—and suddenly remembering those cities on the horizon, falling moons, the hordes dancing around witches burning in terrific fires—I lurched away from him; indeed, I lurched with what was almost an audible *snap*.

Now safely away, I was determined to return to the patio and watch the music.

After accepting another drink from the Hararicart, I thought I had caught the flautist through the corner of my eye, though when I turned my head fully to follower her, she had disappeared. But the band was playing. Wishful thinking? My imagination rushing in to fulfill my desires? Had I too much to drink? I would have thought more about this, but then I was suddenly accosted by an elderly fellow in tweeds—moreover with patches at the elbows. He was most anxious to have a word with me. He went so far as to motion as if he meant to pull the drink away from my face. He blurted that he had heard "reports" I had been spotted at the gathering, and now here I was.

"Yeeeeezzz," I slowly intoned, affecting the blasé mien of an accomplished blaségeoisie. I lowered my drink and nodded. He said:

"There is a world of difference between the people generating nanopoems and the people who are seeking them." He spoke with an air of superiority that more than bourgeoned upon the pejorative, and I had a vague sense that *I had just been warned.* He was evidently a critic of the *Ganzheitliches Weltanschauungsprogramm Schule* who was more than usually impressed with his own opinion. Erm, I thought to myself, *maybe* this was who he was. Nevertheless—and feeling somewhat sharpened up by my recent vision of the witch-burning cities, and that good stiff glass of single-malt; moreover, now with a fresh glass of that elixir in my hands—I stood my ground:

"I had always thought so, but when I had heard there was that machine generating poems without any human input whatsoever… Am I justified in asking the publisher *to pay for that?*" I paused, but clearly *not* for an answer. He was staring at me with his superior eyes, pursing the narrow lips of that horizontal mouth of his, like a slit in the face of a wooden fetish, a coarse monkeypod carving of a haughty elder with his raised hand braced dramatically and pivoting at the top of a pretentious thumbstick; an old, skinny, bald, wrinkle-lipped, sand-gray, and fully-self-obsessed prig. His pinched face was a clear and present *notice*, I could see that. I responded appropriately—that is, I mixed everything up—quivering my jaw, stooping slightly, opening my eyes with faux and therefore *mad* anxiety. Was this having the desired effect? I rapidly shook my head to profess my innocence. He seemed to like this, as I felt he would. I continued: "I wonder, if I—"

He cut me off. "There are further divisions you're not aware of. The guilds of sand-rays, critics, dilatants, editors—" he paused to give me, ahem, *the wrinkled lip and sneer of cold command* "—marketeers, feckless publishers, money-grubbing corporations, fawning academics, the clueless public…" As he prattled on with his taxonomy, I wondered if there were nanopoems in the room. Clinging to the carpet, affixed to the walls, crawling on the plants, in the cat's fur…

There was a sort of gleam in his eyes, which, blinking my eyes, I rather understood to be a *glitch* in his eyes. Well, I thought, that's odd. Then, placing his left hand high on his chest and raising his right hand, palm up, like Cicero, or anyway somebody Roman, he recited the following lines:

Damn the Torpedoes and Run the Program!

The file was over fifty megabytes.
Not one nanopoem in the whole thing!
Not even a twinge of disappointment.
Not one lump in the gravy! No lumps? I felt
Vaguely dissatisfied but remained undeterred.
Such, such were the disappointments,
And, as such, are all part of the business,
Such as it is. Part of the routine. Something
Good should surface somewhere. Bound to.
"Run some more, run some more," I ordered.
"Eventually, somebody will get it right..."

Was he mocking me? Hmm. What I had suspected I now fully saw. He was not an important critic but rather what he himself styled a "sand-ray," one of those persons who made *real* poems—and *real* poems as he understood them were made with machines. Anyway, I am not part of that guild. I did not begrudge him his reserve, yclept smugness, and with an abrupt wince I dismissed him and made my way out of the house into a fresh stream of suggestions.

The Burbank orchestra, much to my chagrin, had been replaced by an expensive PA system with a for-hire DJ from Los Angeles. The beautiful flautist was gone, and I noticed many of the guests had changed out of their swimwear and now were wearing t-shirts; and, my goodness, they flaunted baggy trousers pulled half-way down their thighs to expose all manner of colorful boxer shorts. Moreover, they sported tattoos, large neck chains, and had strange metal things in their mouths. Many wore baseball caps set half-way round on their heads with the bills shooting off to one direction or another—all of it producing a most discommodious effect. The aesthetics were beginning to bleed off.

Fortunately, the memory of the beautiful flautist was still fresh. Maybe I could make something out of that, make something *real*.

I reflected.

Where was I, after all? How real was this place? And the flautist…? I blinked my eyes. The glitches were coming more frequently now, and I sensed an increasing sense of separation, a heavier line of demarcation.

Now another elder with a thumbstick was approaching, so I reckoned it was time to make my exit. No bounding cat led the way, and as I stepped off the sand-ray-flagged patio into the sand-ray-flagged desert of a chilly night, I drew the anorak off my shoulders, pushed my arms into the sleeves, first one then the other, and zipped up all the way.

Charles
Platt

Semiautomatic Songs

by Charles Platt

During a period of concussion that forced me to lie around feeling trapped inside my head, I played a mental game, creating strings of four-letter words which had to follow some simple rules:

- Each word consists of four letters.
- Each word differs from the previous word by only one letter.
- No word can be repeated—but,
- The last word must be the same as the first word.

Subsequently, to test my mental faculties, I converted these rules into a simple computer program loaded with a vocabulary of four-letter words that I found online. Then I added a routine to add a preposition, conjunction, or verb after each word. These bridging terms could be of less than four letters, but not more.

I refer to the result as "semiautomatic" because the software required some help from me.

When these strings of single-syllable words are read aloud, the staccato rhythm gives them a funny denunciatory quality. They also have the sense of almost meaning something, but not quite, typical of machine-generated text controlled by very simple rules.

HOPE

hope you
dope and
doze in
daze you
gaze and
gape the
game that
came the
fame will
fade the
fads the
fans the
pans you
pant and
want you
wont you
dont its
done the
dole the
hole of
hope

HEAR

hear the
fear and
bear the
tear its
near and
neat the
nest was
best but
west you
went you
want you
cant so
cast the
cash and
wash the
rash the
gash will
gush some
mush but
must the
rust be
dust the
lust is
lost at
last so
fast in
fact your
face your
fate your
mate is
male a
mole or
mold you
hold or
held its
head will
hear

LIFE

life will
lift but
rift and
riot the
root and
boot will
loot you
lost but
lest your
best is
bust you
must not
muse the
ruse was
rude so
ride in
side dont
hide its
wide your
wife your
life

LOVE

love the
dove the
dope of
hope that
hops with
hips and
lips and
sips and
sins to
sing he
sang the
song so
long so
lone you
lose your
love

LATE

Late for
date with
mate the
mute with
lute did
lure the
pure but
cure his
care to
pare the
rare and
bare but
fare and
face saw
fate was
late

Five-Letter Versions

When using
five-letter words, it is
much more difficult
to follow the rule of
changing only one
letter in each line,
without running into
a dead end.

LANDS

lands of
sands in
bands she
bends her
beads she
bears she
sears the
scars I
scare and
scale the
shale then
share the
shore a
spore a
sport a
spurt it
spurs and
sours she
soars and
roars she
rears and
reads and
rends and
mends and
lends the
lands

SPACE

space is
spare you
share so
shake the
snake and
snare or
snore on
shore a
whore is
whole but
whose are
those who
chose to
close or
clone a
crone the
crane you

crank and
crack will
track the
trick so
thick you
think it
thins your
chins and
shins it
spins your
spine the
spice of
space

DREAM

dream of
cream a
creak a
break the
bread I
dread my
dream

British writer J. G. Ballard was a regular contributor to *New Worlds* magazine during the 1960s, before his semiautobiographical novel *Empire of the Sun* earned international acclaim in 1984. Ballard used to write short stories in a telegraphic, condensed format, and for one of them, "The Summer Cannibals," I created collages to illustrate it in *New Worlds*. I also made two collages for his short story "Coitus 80."

Collages were a challenge in those days, as there was no way to scan the original material or resize it. Everything was done with scissors and rubber cement—and when the colored fragments were reproduced in monochrome, the printing process tended to gray the highlights and muddy the shadows. I tried to restore some of the tonal range in the versions reproduced here.

—Charles Platt

Coitus 1 – Charles Platt

Coitus 2 – Charles Platt

Jardine
Libaire

Double Tongue

by Jardine Libaire

A few hours ago, around 2am, I snuck into Cari's garage through the unlocked side door. The moon was full and high, flooding the threshold with light and making my target visible: she was zig-zag-marbled cream-and-mahogany, a pit mix, and permanently dirty even though she'd been bathed. The dog was curled on an old lawn-chair cushion whose floral pattern had been bleached into near inexistence by the Mojave sun. Six puppies, still blind and pink-mouthed, nestled in the cove of their mother. Man, I was so fucking amped, adrenaline shot through me like lightning, my skin popped with sweat. I was dead-set. Nothing else to do. Tunnel vision.

I raised the gun, an Ithaca Model 37 with a spreader choke that my late uncle used in Vietnam, I hadn't touched it since the Civil Conflict ended last April—wait, how did I even get to Cari's house? Did I walk through the starlit desert? I live a half mile away. I didn't drive, right? Who cares. Nothing mattered at that moment. Except for pulling the stock to my shoulder, pushing the safety off, and taking aim at the animal—and—

Okay, jesus, goddamn. Slow down. I'm a mess. I'm back home now, I walked, and it's almost dawn. I cut the electricity, turned off my phone, and lit a kerosene lantern on my back porch so I can do this. So I can do this with no signals or service interfering. What exactly am I doing? Writing. I'm writing these words, with *my* hand, mine. When I was a kid, there was only one meaning to *I wrote this by hand*. Handwritten meant hand-fucking-written.

Look. Whoever's reading this, just know you're meeting me at a strange moment. I'm usually chill, I blend in, I stand back. At work, they called me Doo-wop Derek because I wear cardigan sweaters and pomade my hair to the side and always come off old-fashioned-polite. Until now. I'm a disaster. I'm not even sure what's coming out of my pen and showing up on the page but apparently this has to happen.

The world is still dark with night, but the clouds are lining up for a sunrise of velvet cherry-red ink—you need a canvas. I look at the line of lavender on the horizon and know the kind of daybreak that's coming.

Focus, explain what happened.

Cari Bennet. Executive Director of Tomorrow's Today, a nonprofit that coordinates shelter and food for those in need (and after these last eight disrupted years, starting with the pandemic, that count is high). Cari is—was—also my redheaded left-handed boss for the past ten years, the wife of Kevin Bennet, the mother of two teenagers, my secret lover and my beloved. My everything. We made it a decade, undiscovered. We lasted through the vax fights and morgue trucks, the 2025 labor strikes, and the Civil Conflict last year. We seemed unbreakable.

The way she looked at me in meetings: *Jeff, do you have anything to add?* Her eyes empty, trained to look official—that almost made me more excited than when we were alone and she looked at me in a different way, and she whispered, and held me close, and we were right and good.

Her body at work was always trussed and belted, tucked in and restrained in skirt suits, fake gold earrings, pantyhose, tipsy wedge sandals with her plump heels hanging off the backs. But then—when revealed—in the back seat of my car or in the janitor's closet or at the motel down the hill—the curves of her were pale and lavish and desperate. She demanded two rounds each time. She rushed the first, always on top, and cried at the peak, and then the second was slow and she spoiled me. I would do anything for her. We talked incessantly about the day her youngest would finally head off to college and she'd be free, and she'd tell Kevin, and me and her would move to Hawaii.

Anything to add, Jeff?

I never had anything to add, I took what I got, felt grateful I got anything at all, I've always been that kind of guy.

The sun is coming up, the sky ragged with technicolor bands. A rabbit just sprang into sight then vanished.

Keep writing.

Three weeks ago. It imploded. I can't—I still can't believe it. A conference in Riverside, a bunch of us from Tomorrow's Today took three cars, I rode with Robbie and Josephine. We were given a long lunch break, everyone went their separate ways, and I was going to get

Chipotle and asked Cari as she packed stuff into her tote bag if she wanted something. *I do want something,* she said.

Long sad-ass story short, Robbie caught us in the parking lot of the abandoned bowling alley off the frontage road. He saw her car and worried something happened, it was such a weird place to park. Robbie isn't mean, but he told the wrong person, and it all came crashing down. Negotiations were conducted under the table, I got a severance deal, Cari got to stay on as Director, the organization was saved from scandal as everyone signed an NDA. I barely remember that part. I was stunned into disbelief. And I just thought we'd continue, me and Cari, even if I didn't work there anymore. But she refused my calls, she looked past me when I ran into her at Vons, and when I finally got her alone in the parking lot of Tomorrow's Today, she said she'd call the police if I approached her again. *What's done is done*, she said.

I was out of a lover, and unemployed, and 48 years old. I'd never entertained the idea of anyone but Cari, and had been waiting patiently, never thinking, not once, not even close, that we wouldn't end up together. The idea of our future is what got me through all the madness and loss of this decade.

The morning sun is visible. February in the high desert means the sun is welcome. I have a quartz rock holding down the pages I've written so far, and my hand hurts, but I'm not done.

Let's just say I'm not exactly the therapy type. I have no confidantes. Me and my few buddies skirt around the personal—we talk politics, rattlesnake sightings, car engines. So when I finally understood that what was done was, in fact, *done,* I couldn't get out of bed for three days. I had no way to process it. I see that now.

So I went drinking, which is not usually my thing. Hit the Bobcat Bar off 62. It was a rinky-dink joint built in what used to be a dentist office pre-Civil Conflict, and it was impersonal, and it was close enough to stumble home. I got incoherent, stupid, poisonous drunk. Over and over, for a week straight. They had a typical Post-CC selection, from high-dollar Japanese stout to vodka in a plastic bottle, thanks to an infinitely erratic supply chain. On the seventh evening, as I took my stool like it was my job, the lady who chain-smoked and flipped grilled cheeses, the one who'd been watching me, came out of the kitchen. Her long, stringy hair was white with yellow-ish stains, and she had a bronze eyetooth. Barefoot, she wore a different psychedelic kaftan every night.

"Mind if I sit, child?" she asked.

"Course not."

We sat in silence for one drink, then I bought her another.

She knocked it back and looked into my eyes, put her skeletal hand with rhinestone candy-machine rings onto my forearm. "Sweetheart. There's no shortcut to love, and no detour around grief. You're getting into trouble if you don't know that."

She said a few more things which would take me days to properly 'hear' (since I was blocking out the truth), and then she patted my cheek like a grandmother and went back to the griddle.

I lay in bed the next day, hungover, aware that every cycle of drinking then puking then waking up made me feel much worse. But my state of mind was intolerable. I could hardly stand to breathe. My brain was stuck on three thoughts, and I went round and round: 1.) *but she always said she hated Kevin.* 2.) *but what about Hawaii?!* 3.) *why the hell did we pick the bowling alley parking lot???*

Call it serendipity, but that's the day I turned on my transistor radio and heard Jackson Tigre talking with Bo Coogan about the Feel-Real shops popping up all over the country. Sitting in my kitchen, unable to eat my wet cereal, I leaned in when Tigre mentioned *transcending shitty things in your life at lightning speed, screw the old-school pious principles of organic mourning blah blah,* all that. One life, he was insisting, and it's short, might as well pay to curate your mind as fast and easy (and affordably) as you can.

Bo Coogan agreed. "The mentality has *changed* since the Civil Conflict. Beforehand, right, I watched AI trickle into mainstream culture. People were like, afraid to *death* of it then, right?"

Tigre said, "They were uptight, bro. They had no imagination. Now, with fewer people in charge, we're back to that old wild west vibe a lot of us have been waiting for. This is how ideas thrive. This is how concepts turn into kingdoms, bro, I'm telling the truth."

Bo gave a short laugh. "Hundred percent with you. I'm not part of the fear crew." He now said in a simpering voice: "'Oh no, what if AI has unexpected effects on people, gee whiz?!'" He went back to his normal cadence: "Um, people, that's called the nature of existence, right? Life is jampacked with the unexpected repercussions of anything and everything. Nobody's in control—*ever*. Not of nature, not of humanity, not of destiny, and not of AI."

"Bro, so on point," said Tigre. "Which is why I invested in Feel-Real, they're making shit available to the average dude, which is how things should roll."

"Hundred percent," said Bo. "Heard they opened one in Kansas last week."

"Born in N-Y-C, going worldwide, like, immediately."

One opened in Palm Desert last month. I'd seen the billboards: *Feel real good real real fast. Just Ask AI.* Before I knew it, my metallic-beige Acura was speeding through the mountain pass between Morongo and Desert Hot Springs (or what counted for speeding now, since the highways were pleated and potholed; no more taxes means no road maintenance, fellow citizens, duh). Normally, I stayed away from trends like Feel-Real, but I needed—craved—help.

Hi. I'm still here—just took a break and ate a sandwich. Peanut butter on rye, with a glass of water. Why did it taste so good? Because I'm free finally? I was almost surprised when I went into the kitchen and saw the gun lying on the counter, as if someone else left it there. It's noon, and it feels like I'm writing a book here but I'm not done. Ravens are watching me from the telephone wire.

Okay. Feel-Real shop. Ashamed to admit that I went to the one down the hill every day for two weeks. I slunk in that first morning, must have looked like trash, unbathed, bags under my eyes. Smelled like vomit and Listerine. Hair greased back. Cardigan mis-buttoned.

The saleslady was in her forties, maybe? A glossy black mullet but the suburban-mom kind from the 1980s. A tight T-shirt that said *Feel Real* across giant fake tits, and a perfume of cheap cigarettes and fabric softener.

"Ring the alarm, daddy needs comfort," she said, grinning wildly.

"What's that?" I said, caught off-guard.

"Call me Stella."

"Hi Stella," I said.

She smiled conspiratorially. "Don't take this wrong but you look like Mister Rogers after a crack bender. Just kidding!" Before I knew it, she was standing next to me, her arm looped through mine. Said she'd fix me up. When she tried to guess at my heartache—"let me see, job problems? Breakup? Adult loneliness?"

I said: "Yes."

"Oh baby, you're in the right place. Let's tour the facility. Okay?"

We were suddenly walking around the giant round room. Must have been a car dealership Pre-CC, but now it was full of makeshift booths and stalls.

"Aphrodisiac-Attack," she said, pointing to a vending machine. "Sort of like a popper from the 1970s, if you've heard of them? Half hour then it wears off? You lust after whoever you look at right at the moment of ingestion. Makes a boring work shift go fast, for example, and I can vouch for that, if you know what I mean. Whatcha think, daddy?"

How could that help? And the thought of wanting anyone but Cari was offensive. Some part of me wondered if coming here was a mistake. "Um, no thanks."

"That is *quite* all right," she said in a soothing voice, "we got plenty of options."

We looked at the Phuck-Phobia rooms; "we have six of them," she bragged. Four were occupied. We peeked into an empty one: padded walls and a wireless VR headset. Guests take foxy-methoxy—I asked what that was and she said a synther, in the tryptamine class, and I still had no idea what she meant. The client waits till the drug hits, then an AI Friend talks to them through the headset and guides their swarming, distorted, hallucinating brain through a VR landscape of whatever they fear—tarantulas, childhood abuse, war—to create a new experience.

"Shoot, uh—don't think that's for me."

Next stop looked like an old-fashioned hair salon with no barber. Guests put on the medical mask (reminded me of Kabuki) and the AI Facialist evaluates their skin and applies Botox, fillers, or exosomes, which are (she stopped to read a laminated card while chewing her gum madly) "a regenerative thingamajig, something I can't pronounce." She laughed, grabbing my forearm like she'd fall over if she didn't.

I was starting to strategize bowing out when we hit the Suggestive Diary desk. Why did this *immediately* seem like the solution? Because it looked innocent, and reminded me of grade-school homework? After telling the AI Friend my struggles and giving a handwriting sample, I sat at a Lucite desk and put on a beanie with electrodes. Stella slipped me a Style Options pamphlet.

There was a catalog of writers: I could journal like James Baldwin (searing, noble, meticulous) or Mieko Kawakami (radical, intimate, profound), or JG Ballard (dystopian, psychosexual, exotic) or Anne Sexton (cold, lugubrious, sensual)—and there were more abstract choices, like Shy Tween, or Deadpan Homicidal Housewife, or Visionary Passerby, etc.—the list was long, I told her to just choose for me. She had me huff from a pink gas mask, said it was oxidized dopamine and other unnamed chemicals. Then I stuffed my hand into a hard glove attached to a pen, and AI 'helped' me 'write my diary.'

It really felt like I was writing, like I was coming up with the sentences. It *was* my handwriting. But the content was supposedly generated from a machine. I don't remember what I wrote, and it was erased the second the session was done, but I recall lollipops, a red Cadillac, blow jobs, Simpsons reruns, bumblebees, self-love, a toy horse. (Later, I'd try to guess the Style, but came up emptyhanded). However it worked, whatever new tech tactic or invention this Suggestive Diary hijacked, I did not give the slightest fuck—I'd gone from suicidal to giddy and floating and hopeful. It made no sense, but the effect was undeniable. My soul had been grabbed by its shoulders and turned in a new direction.

Before I left the building, I made an appointment for the next day. I tried to get another session right then and there, but they said it couldn't be done more than once daily.

"Oh yeah, papa bear, I knew you'd dig it," Stella said as she held the door open for me, and she squinted into the sun and waved as I got in my car.

The whole ride home, then walking into my living room, throwing my keys on the coffee table, sitting on my couch—I waited to be invaded by the pain, the rumination. Nothing. It's like I was in a plexiglass bubble. Bad thoughts died like bugs on the windshield. Smashed, blown away. How was that possible? My consciousness was fixed. I rang up my buddies and we met for tacos, talked about NetMax shows, rain, the Middle East. No need to get wasted. When I woke up the next day, thoughts of Cari circled my consciousness like faraway vultures, and that scared me, so I grabbed a banana for breakfast and drag-raced to the low desert.

Stella hugged me, mashing her breasts between us, and led me to the desk like we were heading to a bedroom. Very casually, over her shoulder, she asked if there were any, you know, *odd* feelings or incidents since yesterday's "sesh."

"Yes. Odd as in, I was free from despair," I joked.

"Yay yay yay! Always gotta ask 'bout side-effect actions, but come on, mister, I don't think so, you know?" With that mostly senseless statement, she plugged me in to the pink gas. As she left me to my notebooking, she singsonged: “FYI, we *do* permit tipping, if you dig the outcome of our service, just saying!” She winked and vanished.

I couldn’t start writing fast enough, and it was a blur, and then it was done, and I walked out (giving Stella a twenty) high as a kite on random poetic observations and who-knows-what kind of neurological engineering. Got home. Heated up a pizza. Watched something about barrier reefs on PBS. And then I was lying in bed, reading a magazine and about to sign off, whistling, no less, because why not, when my vision darkened. My blood was heating up. Not emotionally—physically. So hot that I tore off my pajamas and lay there, panting. Visions skipped through my head, random, bizarre, disturbing—me stepping on a kangaroo rat, tearing flowers off a desert willow, knocking two kids’ heads together on the bus. The heat and the state of being passed after ten minutes, and I tried to forget it.

My eyes are dry from filling these looseleaf pages, my hand aches. It’s afternoon, I’ve moved into my living room. Sitting cross-legged on the concrete floor and writing at the coffee table. I’m not stopping till it’s completed.

Went straight to Feel-Real the next morning. Stella greeted me like her best friend, while she leered at a pimply teenager stocking shelves—she must have gotten into the aphrodisiacs. She forgot to ask about side effects, but I didn’t care that she didn’t care, and I didn’t bring up the heat or the aggro hallucinations. I did the session. Left flush with good vibes, waving to Stella. It wasn't until I was home, the late afternoon shining milky-blue. I went out to prune my palo verde, and suddenly got cramps and doubled over. A pit of fervor exploded in my ribs, like a grease fire, and I think I hyperventilated.

But that's not even the real problem. It's that this propelled me somehow, as if sleepwalking, to—*listen to this*—pick up a half-desiccated bird corpse I'd noticed earlier, a few maggots still attached, and march around front to stick it in my neighbor's mailbox. It wasn't done as a prank. I was seething with hatred. Hatred for a neighbor I honestly liked, we had no beef at all. When I came back to reality, I was in my kitchen, and I had to lie down.

In bed, under the sheets, hiding, I suddenly heard the Bobcat Bar lady, whispering to me like a ghost. *You have to feel the sorrow, you have to know what you lost, go for long walks and cry, lie awake all night and curse the world. You have to look in the mirror and be devastated by what you see. You have to believe for a moment that this is the end of everything good. If you adore someone, you have to live through it. You have to be confused. You have to live without security, without assurance. You have to be brave, not fearless. You have to live without knowing why all the time, so one day you can know again. And if you don't do these things, it will all go wrong, and come out in bad ways, in very bad ways, indeed.*

I closed my eyes tight and counted to a hundred, trying to shut her up, and I eventually slept.

It's possible my eyes grazed a headline in the *Certified Gazette* about a class action suit against Feel-Real, but I didn't read further. My mind had one track: I wanted to be soothed. Come morning, I beelined for Feel-Real, stood at the front doors as they unlocked them for the day. Stella and I barely chatted anymore, she just set me up to "write" while talking on her cell or flirting with whatever underage cashier she'd traded Aphrodisiac Attacks with. I always left with a beatific smile. And I always did something violent in the evening.

One night, I set fire to a rolled newspaper and held it up in the evening breeze, watching cinders fly into dry creosote, waiting for 29 Palms to burn. Nothing happened, but still. *What the fuck was that?!*

"Maybe I should understand this procedure just, like, a little bit better?" I said to Stella that day before my session. "Is it…creating new memories for me?"

"Not quite." Stella bit into her microwaved burrito.

"Then—are new patterns of thinking being produced?"

"Sort of," she said, mouth full.

"Is it erasing memories or thoughts, or—can you just explain it a tad?"

"It's a mixture, it's totally everything you said."

I must have looked dissatisfied because she resorted to reciting some training language in a robotic way: "Suggestive Diary success is brought about by introducing new thoughts, reorganizing existing ones, deleting certain old thoughts, but also—at the same exact time—

creating *emotion* by combining neuron stimulation, chemicals, and creative material that seems self-generated. The last element is essential because if it didn't seem self-produced, the diary session would be ineffective."

I hesitated, but ultimately, I sat down at the desk, put the beanie on, slipped the hand into the glove. Later that afternoon, I was looking on NeighborHood to see if anyone had advice for dealing with spider mites on a honey mesquite tree when I saw a post by Cari, and I looked at her page. It was almost an adventure to look at her profile and not feel anything. Like I was holding my finger in a candle's flame but felt nothing. I read her posts. The week before she'd apparently found a pregnant dog in her yard, starving. She announced she was keeping her. Cari was always giddy, over the moon, about strays. She then posted about the birth. *Who wants puppies?!!? Get on the list. OMG, I'm in love with this Mama, she's a survivor!!*

That night, I was at Aki Sushi, totally sober, and I went up to a random table and snatched a lady's wine glass and smashed it on the floor. The next morning, I woke up and found a painting of sand dunes, a watercolor I inherited from my grandfather, slashed with a knife and lying on the floor. I remembered these things like they were dreams, not like things I'd done. Dreams welded over the blaze of hostility.

It's evening now, by the way. I'm back on the porch, breathing cool night air, and I'm near the finish-line. What will happen after I write the last word here? No idea. Coogan and Tigre were at least correct in stating that we don't, we can't, control everything. Or anything.

Did I stop my Suggestive Diary appointments? I did not. I plowed on, session after session, inhaling the oblivion it doled out, even though at night I'd get fever attacks. I'd do things. I'd glare like a child from a horror movie with red-rimmed eyes and a toothy grin as I keyed a car probably on lease to some poor soul in college, or I'd curveball a rock at a stranger across the road. Implosions of antagonism. I carved nasty words into the bathroom stall door. Words I theoretically didn't believe in. Looking back now, I'm horrified that my own comfort was so wonderful that these "side-effect actions" didn't slow me down let alone stop me. It was also heartbreaking that I didn't spend a minute thinking about what actually happened with Cari. How our chaos might have hurt her kids. How I left my clients at Tomorrow's Today without saying goodbye. I feel sick now thinking about it.

That Feel-Real shop—I'll never forget it and will never set foot in that shit-palace again, that room that stank of chemicals and drive-through cheeseburgers and drywall and steel and dirty dollar bills. After the scene in Cari's garage, I'm done. And as the stars blink and shimmer above me, I thank fucking heavens I'm also at the last page. My wrist feels broken, but I'm about to sign off and fold these pages and stash them in a drawer.

I just have to explain what happened in the garage, how the stock of the shotgun was pulled hard to my shoulder, my eye sighting down the barrel and seeing the dog's creamy chest move with her breath, her jowls twitching, the pups slick and whimpering around her nipples, and I put my finger on the cold metal trigger.

When I walked home early this morning, the sand moonlit in an otherworldly way, the gun broken over my forearm, it came to me like an order from my own heart: when I get home, I will write down—by myself, with no machines—why I *didn't* pull the trigger. Because I didn't. I was kneeling on that garage floor, but instead of firing, I caught my breath, my eyes wet, and suddenly cracked the gun. Popped the shells. Write down why I exhaled, then almost yelped in fear, realizing what I might have done—why I stood up, blurry, blood rushing to my head—and I backed away, stumbling as if drunk, even though I wasn't drunk, leaving the mother and her litter unharmed, giving and drinking milk. I left them in the desert night. Why? Write it down so I never go near the machines again and so I never forget: it was life, I saw life in the spangled amber eyes of the dog, and *life saw me.*

Empty Spaces – Jacques Garnier

Mark

Soden Jr.

A Short History of Parking Structures

by Mark Soden Jr.

The transition from the city center to the suburbs is marked by many things. The metric we are using for this discussion is parking.

In the era after World War II houses were built at a dizzying rate of speed. Developers were more concerned that they might run out of catchy street names, than wondering if they had buyers for the little houses that they were throwing together. The plan included a supermarket and gas station. Sure, there were sewers, water and electricity, but after that the developer was off the hook to provide for the people that invested in these dwellings.

So how do you lure people to buy houses far removed from the density, culture and opportunity that cities offer? Parking is the key.

Even the most modest, poorly stocked market would have an ocean of asphalt as a parking lot in front. In winter to sell Christmas Trees and in the summer to sell Fireworks. Parking is the natural resource that city centers lack. Free parking in large quantities works in a society where people love their cars more than other people.

In time, the equation changed between parking and real estate. It was no longer possible to commit vast two-dimensional areas to parking. If you could commit a third of the space and start stacking the levels above it … Once again, the experience of massive free parking can be achieved.

Let us begin the short history of the parking structure, most of this has been looted from the internet. So, the "Facts" can be sort of … flexible. I would suggest that you accept this new low in research and reporting as "the new normal" and we will simply move on with the narrative.

"The earliest known multi-story car park was opened in May 1901 by City & Suburban Electric Carriage Company at 6 Denman Street, central London. The location had space for 100 vehicles, over seven floors, totaling 19,000 square feet. The same company opened a second location in 1902 for 230 vehicles. The company specialized in the sale, storage, valeting and on-demand delivery of electric vehicles that could travel about 40 miles and had a top speed of 20 miles per hour."

The City & Suburban Electric Carriage Company adventure in electric vehicles pre-dates the opening of the Tesla Factory in Fremont California by one hundred and fourteen years. The only aspect of City & Suburban Electric Carriage Company that made history is the parking structure.

"Built between 1898 and 1906 in Barcelona, Spain, Casa Batlló is the house of the Dragon with its delightful stained-glass windows, a winding roof-back: colorful as a rainbow. Casa Batlló is known for another innovation – the first underground parking anywhere. Designed by the Iconic Architect Antoni Gaudi, it is remarkable for any parking design for its interior below-grade circular helix built in 1904."

If you are looking for an architect that will solve a problem as artistically as possible, look no further than Antoni Gaudi. Till I did this "research" I had no idea that Antoni Gaudí was on the vanguard of solving our parking problem.

"The earliest known parking garage in the United States was built in 1918 for the Hotel La Salle at 215 West Washington Street in the West Loop area of downtown Chicago, Illinois. It was designed by Holabird and Roche. The Hotel La Salle was demolished in 1976, but the parking structure remained because it had been designated as preliminary landmark status and the structure was several blocks from the hotel. It was demolished in 2005 after failing to receive landmark status from the city of Chicago."

Isn't it just like a bureaucrat to decide, that although it was the first parking garage in the county, and that it had been there for 87 years that it was not significant and it needed to come down. These are the sort of decisions that lead the world to think. "Americans don't value their history."

Parking, like so many uses of space, is a rental agreement. A place to park a valuable asset for a period of time. An hourly rates motel for your car. Perhaps we could extend this rental concept a bit farther. With the addition of a couple of upscale porta-potties your parking structure could become a "campground" from 10 PM to 7 AM. Then you could still rent it to cars during the day.

There is a church in my town that built the parking structure first. For a period of time they were having services in a tent. Eventually they built a church. I still refer to them as "The First Church of the Parking Structure." As we say, "First Things, First." And that is just how important parking is.

* https://en.wikipedia.org/wiki/Multistorey_car_park

- Listen to the Phog Masheeen audio version of this article at https://tinyurl.com/P-structure

Tenants Only – Jacques Garnier

Pacific Life – Jacques Garnier

www.ingramcontent.com/pod-product-compliance
Lightning Source LLC
Chambersburg PA
CBHW011144310726
48972CB00009B/2853

* 9 7 9 8 9 8 9 6 3 0 8 2 0 *